Animal Homes

Written by Natalie Tucker

STECK-VAUGHN
C O M P A N Y

A Division of Harcourt Brace & Company

www.steck-vaughn.com

Animals live in all kinds of homes.
Some animals live underground.
Some animals live high in the mountains.
Others live in the tops of trees or deep
in the water.

Moles live in tunnels underground. The tunnels are called burrows. Moles make leaf beds to sleep on. They spend most of their lives in their burrows.

Rabbits live underground, too.
They dig holes to make their homes.
Their homes are called warrens.
Rabbits put grass and leaves inside.
Sometimes several rabbit families live
together in a warren.

Eagles usually live in the mountains.
They build their nests in tall trees.
Baby eagles are safe up in the treetops.
Every year, eagles add new branches to
their old nest.
Some nests get very big.

Koalas live in trees in Australia.
They spend all their time in the trees.
They get their food and water there.
Koalas only come down when they have
to move to another tree.

Beavers live in rivers, streams, or lakes.
They cut down trees with their sharp
front teeth.
They use the trees to build their homes.
Their homes are called lodges.
Beavers enter them under the water.

Many frogs live in ponds.
They stay in the water most of the time.
When the water is very cold, frogs go
to the bottom of the pond.
They cover themselves with the mud
there to keep warm.

Animals can live in other places, too.
Bears and bats live in caves.
Foxes live in dens.
Some animals even live in our homes.
They are our pets.